Mr. Lucky Straw
Rewritten by Elizabeth Lane
Illustrated by Hala Day

One day a poor farmer named Yosaku was walking down the road.

He tripped over a stone and tumbled head over heels into a mud puddle. "What good fortune!" he exclaimed, sitting up. "I could have landed on the hard ground and been hurt! Instead I have fallen into this nice, soft mud! It was meant to be! This is my lucky day!"

As he brushed himself off, Yosaku noticed a piece of straw stuck to his sleeve. He started to throw the straw away. Then he stopped to think, "If this is my lucky day, maybe this is a lucky straw. I will save it."

As Yosaku went on down the road,
a dragonfly started buzzing around his head.

“Shoo! Go away!”

Yosaku batted at the dragonfly.

But the pesky insect would not leave, so Yosaku took a string and tied the dragonfly to the end of the straw.

Soon he met a woman and a little boy. “Mama!” shouted the little boy. “Look at that dragonfly tied to a straw! I want it! Please get it for me!”

"You need it more than I do," said Yosaku. He gave the dragonfly and the straw to the little boy.

The woman was so grateful that she gave Yosaku three of the oranges she was carrying.

“What lovely oranges!” said Yosaku.

“And all because I saved a piece of straw! This is my lucky day!”

Soon Yosaku met a peddler with a heavy load of cloth. “I’m so hot and thirsty!” the peddler sighed. “One of those oranges would be delicious!”

"You need the oranges more than I do. You can have them all," said Yosaku. He gave the peddler all three of the oranges. The peddler was so grateful that he gave Yosaku three pieces of fine silk cloth.

"What lovely cloth!" said Yosaku. "And all because I saved a piece of straw! This is my lucky day!" Soon Yosaku met a princess. She was traveling in a covered litter with her guards and servants.

"What beautiful cloth!" she said when she saw Yosaku. "Just what I need for my new kimono! Would you let me have a piece?"

"You need the cloth more than I do. You can have it all," said Yosaku. He gave the princess all three pieces of cloth. The princess was so grateful that she gave Yosaku a big bag of gold.

Yosaku walked home to his village carrying the gold.

He saw some poor, hungry people in their huts.

"They need this gold
more than I do," he said.

Yosaku used the gold to buy land for all the people in his village. Now they could raise their own food. No one would go hungry.

"And all because I saved a piece of straw!" said Yosaku.
"This was truly my lucky day!"
The people in Yosaku's village were very happy.
And after that, they always called Yosaku "Mr. Lucky Straw."